This book belongs to

_____

_____

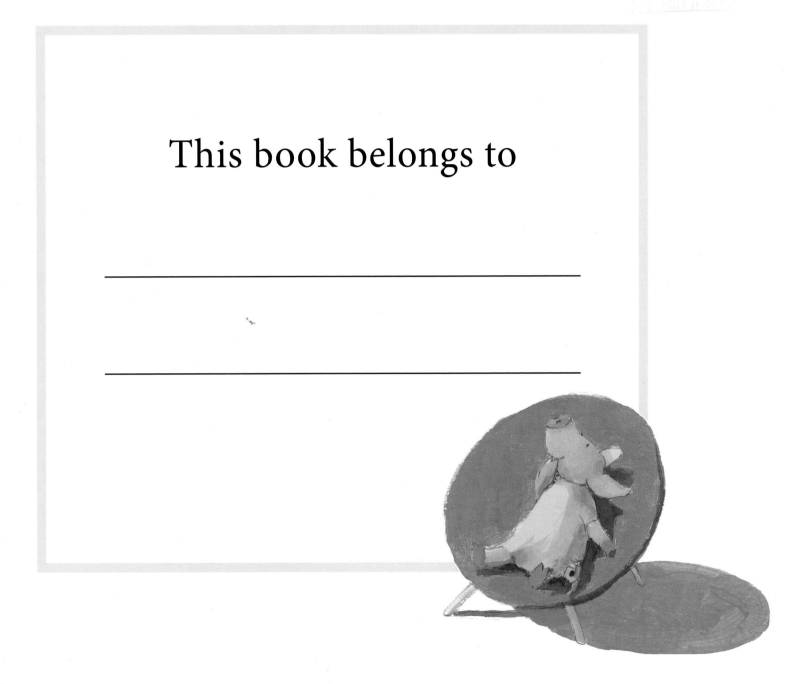

For Dennis, Christine, Mark, Elsie and Jim . . .

C.A.

This edition published by Albury Books in 2014
Albury Court, Albury, Thame, Oxfordshire, OX9 2LP, United Kingdom

Text © Claire Alexander | Illustrations © Claire Alexander
The rights of Claire Alexander to be identified as the author and illustrator of
this work has been asserted by her in accordance with the Copyright, Designs
and Patents Act 1988

ISBN 978-1-910235-51-4 (hardback)
ISBN 978-1-910235-62-1 (paperback)

A CIP Catalogue Record for this title is available from the British Library

Printed in China

Small Florence

CLAIRE ALEXANDER

Albury Books

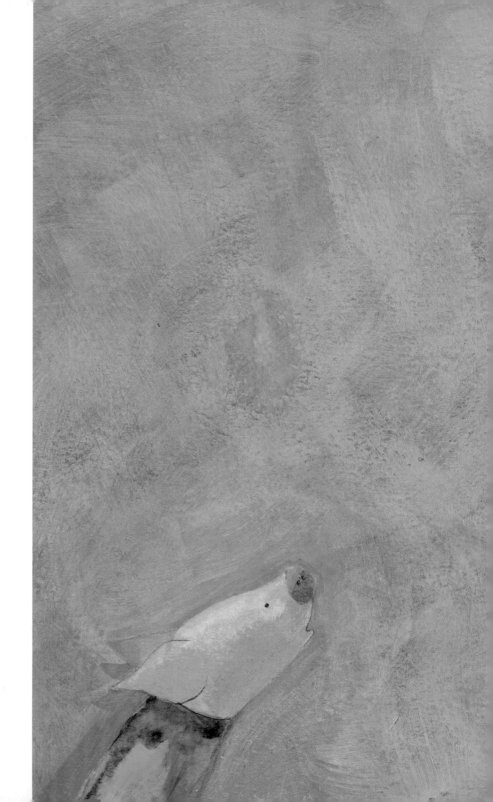

Florence was a small pig.
She was a happy soul,
if a little shy at times.

She had two older sisters.

What's small, pink and squeaky?

Florence!

Florence thought her sisters were very lucky. They were taking singing lessons from Jazzy-Funk Mutt, the cool singing teacher.

Ham it up, sisters
Smooth!

Florence dreamed of
one day becoming a piggy
pop star on television.

She sang to herself in secret. She sang under the covers of her bed at night and she sang in the bath every morning.

After a while, she plucked up the courage to sing to her friends . . .

One evening, there was an announcement on the TV. **SINGING COMPETITION!** The **WINNER** will perform live on **TELEVISION!**

"Let's enter the competition!" squealed Florence's sisters as they started rummaging through their wardrobes for costumes to wear.

"Can I sing with you in the competition?" asked Florence. "YOU!" snorted the sisters, "YOU can sing? Go on then, sing us a song right now!"

Florence took
a deep breath, raised
her head and opened her little
snout. But as she looked up, she saw
her big sisters peering down at her. Suddenly,
she felt very small, and very, very shy, and very, very,
very nervous. And all she could manage was a teeny, tiny . . .

"Squeak!"

Every day she asked her
sisters if she could join
their singing practice, but
every day they said
"No."
All Florence could do was
listen to them rehearse.
Soon she knew all the words
front to back and back to
front and inside out.

Finally the day of the competition arrived . . .

TELEVISION STUDIOS

The queue outside the television studios
stretched for miles and miles.

At last the doors opened, and the first band played their song. The judges looked impressed and the crowd cheered. Florence waited excitedly for her sisters to appear . . .

You are my catawall

She waited and waited . . .   and waited . . .   and waited some more . . .

until finally . . .

Florence's sisters burst
onto the stage singing
with all their might. But as
they sang they looked out into the . . .

large crowd
and they started to feel

very small

Then they looked up and saw
the . . .

TV cameras.
And they suddenly felt
very, very shy. And when
their eyes met with
the . . .

beady eyes of the
judges they felt so
nervous they forgot all
the words to their song!
Everything went quiet. . .

until a small voice
started singing from
the crows.
"Find that voice!"
shouted the judges

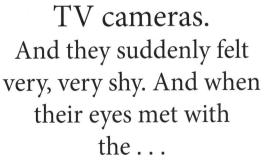

The search-light went out over
the crowd, and guess who it found?

A small pink pig standing on
tip-toe, now singing with all her might!

"Please take to the stage,
little pig!" called the judges.

Florence's sisters were
not laughing at her now.

And as she trotted up to the stage,
Florence did not feel small, or shy or nervous.

Florence was awarded First Prize.
And her dream of becoming a
piggy popstar was about to come true.

Florence topped the charts with songs about love, life and vegetarianism. And as for her sisters, they never sang again, but they made sure all their friends knew just who their little sister was!

That's our sister

we taught her everything she knows!

MUSIC SHOP

MUSIC SHOP

No. 1

Small Florence